Mermaids
TO THE RESCUE

Lana Swims North

ALSO BY LISA ANN SCOTT

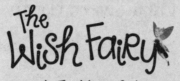

Mermaids TO THE RESCUE

The Wish Fairy

ENCHANTED PONY ACADEMY

Mermaids
TO THE RESCUE

Lana Swims North

Lisa Ann Scott

illustrated by
Heather Burns

SCHOLASTIC INC.

Text copyright © 2019 by Lisa Ann Scott
Illustrations by Heather Burns, © 2019 Scholastic Inc.

All rights reserved. Published by Scholastic Inc., *Publishers since 1920.* SCHOLASTIC and associated logos are trademarks and/or registered trademarks of Scholastic Inc.

ISBN 978-1-338-26700-6

10 9 8 7 6 5 4 3 2   19 20 21 22 23

Printed in the U.S.A.   40

First printing 2019

Book design by Yaffa Jaskoll

To A.M.—Aren't you so glad
narwhals are real?

Chapter 1

Princess Lana sat at her desk at the Royal Mermaid Rescue Crew School, tapping her pencil. She couldn't stop thinking about their assignment: how to rescue five stranded sea turtles at once. She looked out the window at the fish swimming by as she searched for an answer.

"Lana, what do you think?" Principal Vanora asked.

Suddenly, she got a great idea. "I could put them all on a raft and pull them to safety!"

Some of the other merchildren and seaponies in class laughed. Even some of the younger first-year students chuckled.

The principal swished her sparkly blue tail and adjusted her hair. "What are you talking about?"

Lana blinked a few times. "To rescue the turtles," she said quietly.

The principal frowned. "That's a fine answer for our homework assignment, but right now, we're studying jellyfish. I asked which one is the most dangerous. And the answer is the box jellyfish. It's one of the most deadly in all the seas."

Lana sunk down in her seat. She wanted

to disappear, which wasn't easy with her pink-streaked hair. She fiddled with the hem of her shirt.

"Please pay closer attention, Lana," the principal said.

Lana nodded and bit her lip.

Her magical seapony partner, Marina, smiled nicely. "The raft was a great idea," she whispered.

"Thanks." Lana loved being a Rescue Crew member, but sometimes it was hard to stay focused. There was so much to learn and remember. And her classmates were some of the smartest, bravest merkids in the sea. Lana wanted to impress them all, but whenever she got the courage to speak up, she usually embarrassed herself.

"Anyone know what the biggest jellyfish in the world is?" the principal asked.

Lana remembered studying a species from the Northern Seas called the lion's mane jellyfish. Its tentacles could be over one hundred feet long! But she didn't dare speak up now after bungling the last question.

"It's the lion's mane jellyfish," Princess Cali said.

"Very good," the principal said.

Lana frowned, wishing she had been the one who'd impressed the principal.

"Now, to help you identify the many types of jellyfish, I want you each to draw a picture of five different species by the end of the month," Principal Vanora said.

"Hello? I need help!" A call came in through the rescue shells each crew member wore around his or her neck. The calls always reached the crew members closest to the emergency. Today, it was the children in the Rescue Crew School.

"Princess Nixie, why don't you respond," the principal said.

Lana was glad she didn't have to answer the call in front of everyone. Nixie was so brave. She'd already been on a mission by herself and saved her two best friends from a shark!

Nixie picked up her rescue shell and spoke into it. "This is the Rescue Crew. What's the problem?"

"My little merboy, Nico, is missing. He was at the park, but now we can't find him!"

"Stay there. We'll meet you at the park," Nixie told the worried mermother.

"Class, we should all go and help," the principal said.

"Even the first years?" asked Drake, the youngest of the royal merstudents.

"We need everyone's help, and it'll be good practice for the day you're sent on a mission alone," the principal said.

Lana was surprised. This was the first time the whole class was going on a real call. Usually, just a few crew members responded to an emergency. But a missing merchild was a very serious situation.

The students swam out of the school, through the city. They headed toward the park at the edge of the capital city of Astoria.

"I hope I can help find him," Lana whispered to Marina.

"You've got this. Remember what we say in class?" Marina asked.

Lana nodded. "Breathe, focus, solve."

Lana heard the merboy's parents and a few merchildren calling for him. "Nico! Where are you?"

"Cali and Cruise, you're the lead members on this rescue," Principal Vanora said.

"Got it!" The twin mermaids flicked their shiny silver tails as they swam over to the missing merboy's family.

"Tell us what happened," Cali said.

"We were playing hide-and-seek in the park," a mergirl said, "and we told Nico to wait on the swings."

"He's only four years old!" his mother said. "You shouldn't have left him alone."

"But he likes the swings," said a merboy. "We thought he'd stay there."

"So what happened after you left him?" Cruise asked.

"We played the game. By the time we found the last merkid hiding, Nico was gone," his sister explained.

"I wonder if he's ever run off before?" Lana quietly asked Marina as they waited off to the side.

"Good question," Marina whispered back.

"Has he ever disappeared before?" Cali asked.

"No, never. He's a very good little merboy," Nico's father said.

"Oh, you have to find him," his mother said.

"We will," Cruise said. "We're the Royal Mermaid Rescue Crew. You can count on us."

Lana stared at the swing set, thinking. Hide-and-seek was a long game. Nico probably got bored. *Where would I go if I were still a little merkid?*

"Okay, there are eight of us," Cali said. "Lana, you'll join Cruise and me with our seaponies to search the park. Dorado and Nixie, take your seaponies and follow the route back to his home to see if he got lost on the way."

Cruise turned to the first-year students. "Drake, Darya, and Waverly, search the areas just outside the park."

"Quickly!" Cali pointed to where they should swim. "He could be injured."

"I hope not—we've just started learning about healing!" Nixie said.

"Let's go!" Dorado said.

The Rescue Crew members swam to their assignments. Lana stayed where she was, thinking.

Cries for the boy filled the air. "Nico? Nico, where are you?"

Cruise and Cali zipped around the park, poking their heads in every hole and crevice.

Maybe he decided to join the game and hide, too? Lana thought. But why wasn't he answering? She snapped her fingers.

"What is it?" Marina asked.

"He probably felt left out. Maybe he joined the hide-and-seek game without them knowing and then fell asleep while hiding!" Lana said.

Marina nodded. "That's a very good theory."

Lana's gaze swept across the park, looking for places a little merboy might hide. "Maybe he's in the garden over there. It would be comfortable, and it's not far from the swings."

As she and Marina looked, Lana noticed that Cruise was on the other side of the park, swimming over to the seaweed garden. Before Lana knew it, he was shouting, "Hey, I think I see something over here."

Everyone rushed to the garden. Lana spotted the tip of a tiny green fin sticking out from under a patch of seaweed. The tail was the same color as the plant.

Cali must've seen it, too. "Look!" She

carefully parted the seaweed. A little merboy was curled up, napping.

"Nico!" The merboy's family scooped him
up, hugging and kissing him.

"We found him!" Cruise hollered.

"Hey, *I* found him," Cali said.

"But I told you where to look," Cruise said.

Cali rolled her eyes.

"We all worked together on this," Principal Vanora said. "Well, almost everyone. And we found the missing merboy. Nicely done."

Nico rubbed his eyes. "Did I win hide-and-seek?"

While everyone laughed, Marina whispered to Lana, "You figured out where he was before anyone else. You should have said something!"

Lana sighed. "I know."

Cali picked up her shell and called the other crew members back to the park.

"Excellent work, class!" Principal Vanora said. "You are dismissed for the day." Then she turned to Lana and her smile fell. "We need to talk."

Chapter 2

While the other crew members swam off to celebrate their successful mission, Lana approached Principal Vanora. "Yes?"

"Why weren't you searching for the boy?" The principal sounded disappointed.

Lana stammered. "But—but I was."

"You didn't move a fin. You stayed in the middle of the park."

Lana's mouth opened and closed a few

times, but nothing came out. Sometimes, it was so hard to find the right words.

The principal sighed. "When an emergency is unfolding, we have to act quickly."

Marina spoke up. "But she—"

The principal held up her hand. "Lana has to speak for herself."

Lana hung her head. "I'm sorry. I'll do better next time."

"I hope so. Until I see some improvements from you, you can't lead a rescue mission," the principal said softly. "I just don't think you're ready."

Lana gasped.

The principal set her hand on Lana's shoulder. "Some crew members need a little more time and work to get the hang of it.

You have one more year of Rescue Crew School. Work your hardest. Ask your partner for help. You're a team now. Remember what we say? 'A team takes two.' You can do this."

Lana nodded, blinking back tears. "I'll try my best."

"Good. I'll see you tomorrow in class."

Principal Vanora swam off, leaving Lana and Marina alone in the park.

"Why didn't you tell her you figured out where Nico was?" Marina asked.

Lana shrugged. "Because it didn't help find him."

"But you were right—and you would have searched the garden if Cruise and Cali hadn't gotten there first," Marina said.

Lana shook her head. "No, I should have been swimming around and looking. I'm a horrible Rescue Crew member."

"You're not!" Marina said. "But you do need to speak up for yourself."

"I don't know how," Lana said. "I get so nervous when I have to talk to the principal. Or in front of the class. And when I do speak, sometimes I say the wrong thing and I get so embarrassed. Like talking about rafts."

"As your partner, I'll just have to keep reminding you how good you really are until you believe it yourself," Marina said.

Despite her sad mood, Lana smiled. She was lucky to have such a kind and thoughtful seapony partner.

Marina nudged Lana with her long snout. "Let's go home and have dinner. Get some sleep. You'll feel better in the morning."

"Let's go for a swim first," Lana said.

Together they swam to the coral gardens at the edge of the kingdom. Lana went there sometimes to daydream.

"Can you use your Sea Savvy to make us blend into the background?" she asked

Marina. "I don't want anyone to see me. I want to be alone for a while."

"Of course. Climb on," Marina said.

All magical seaponies had a special Sea Savvy, and Marina's was wonderful. Lana wrapped her arms around Marina's neck, and they both faded into the colors of the coral behind them, disappearing from view.

Lana sighed. "Maybe I don't belong on the crew."

"You'll find your place," Marina said. "There were times at the Enchanted Seapony Academy when Headmaster Caspian scolded me. I know how you feel."

Lana heard the sound of sniffles and crying.

"Please don't cry," Marina said.

"It's not me!" Lana whispered. She saw something big and dark approaching them. "Look!"

A creature emerged from the shadows. Lana had never seen anything like it.

"What is that?" Marina whispered.

"I don't know!" It was a gray animal, like a dolphin, with a horn coming out of its head. The creature looked so sad, Lana thought it couldn't be dangerous. "Hello?" she called.

The creature stopped. It looked around. "Who's there? Where are you?"

Lana giggled. "Marina, we're still blending in with the background."

"Oops!" Quickly, Marina and Lana reappeared.

"Oh, that's quite a trick!" the creature said.

"Marina's a magical seapony," Lana said. "And we're members of the Royal Mermaid Rescue Crew. Do you need help? Are you lost?"

"I'm not lost, exactly," the creature said. "But I'm not entirely sure where I am."

Lana smiled. "That sounds a little bit like being lost. What's your name?"

"Spike. Because of my . . ." He rolled his eyes up to look at his horn.

"I'm Lana, and this is Marina."

"Where are you from? I've never seen anyone like you," Marina said.

"I live in the Eastern Seas with a pod of dolphins. But I'm the only one with a horn," Spike said.

"How magnificent!" Lana said.

"No, it's not. Some of the dolphins tease me about my horn, of course. But that's not the biggest problem."

"What is?" Marina asked gently.

Spike frowned. "I keep poking other dolphins by mistake. I cut my best friend. He was bleeding!"

"Oh my goodness!" Lana said.

"I can't let that happen again. They're not safe with me," Spike explained. "It's better if I'm on my own. I just don't fit in."

"I know how you feel," Lana said. "All the other Rescue Crew merkids are better at everything than me."

"It's not a good feeling, is it?" Spike asked.

Lana shook her head.

"That's why I'm not lost," Spike said. "I'm searching for a new home. But I don't know where I am."

"We can help you," Lana said. "I live in the kingdom of Stillwater, north of here, but I'm spending the weekend in my dorm at the Rescue Crew School. Stay with us tonight!"

"Oh, thank you," Spike said. "I never thought I'd run into such helpful creatures."

A warm feeling spread through Lana's chest. This is what it was supposed to feel like being a Rescue Crew member. Why couldn't it always feel like this?

Chapter 3

Lana and Marina brought Spike to their room while everyone else was at dinner.

"Let's stay here," Lana said. "I don't want anyone teasing me about what happened in class. I've got kelp cakes. Let's share those."

"I hope you don't get in trouble for having me here," Spike said as they ate.

"As far as I know, there's no rule against letting a dolphin with a horn sleep over!" Marina joked.

"Thank you so much for your kindness," Spike said.

"We keep the seas safe for all creatures," Lana said. "Even ones we've never seen before."

Spike smiled as he fell asleep.

But Lana stayed awake much of the night, wondering how she could fit in better on the Rescue Crew. It would probably be as easy as Spike losing his horn.

Lana woke up early the next day, worried as soon as her eyes opened.

"I hope I don't get in trouble for this," she said to Marina as they swam to class.

"He needs our help. You're doing the right thing," Marina assured her.

"I don't know. I never seem to do the right

thing these days," Lana whispered as she opened the door to the classroom.

Principal Vanora stopped talking. "You're late, Princess Lana."

"I know. I . . . I . . ." She gulped. "I brought a guest. A new friend."

The class gasped as Spike swam in.

"Who is this?" the principal asked.

Lana froze; she was so nervous. So Marina explained how they met.

"I've heard of creatures like you," the principal said to Spike.

"Really?" he said.

She nodded. "But I can't remember your name. You're not a dolphin. You're a very rare animal."

"I am?" Spike sounded amazed. "So I'm not just a mistake?"

"No creature is a mistake," the principal said. "But you're not the only one of your kind."

Spike smiled. "That's wonderful."

"Indeed. But unfortunately, any books that might tell us more about you were swept away from our library during the Great Storm, many years ago."

"I've seen creatures on land with one horn," Marina said. "At the Enchanted Pony Academy. They're called uniponies."

"Maybe you're a uniphin!" Dorado joked.

Spike smiled. "Maybe."

I wonder if the uniponies might know

something about horned creatures of the sea, Lana wondered.

"Hey!" Nixie said. "We should go to the Enchanted Pony Academy and find out what the ponies know about creatures like Spike."

"Excellent idea. Sounds like a good reason for a field trip," the principal said.

Lana sighed. She'd had the very same idea. Why hadn't she been brave enough to share it?

"Marina, since you've been there before, can you lead the class to the academy?" the principal asked.

The class buzzed with excitement. Normally, merchildren weren't supposed to swim to the river.

"I'd love to!" Marina said.

"Come directly back to school and tell me what you've discovered," the principal said.

The class followed Marina and Lana out of the school. Spike swam alongside them.

"Another creature with a horn? I can't wait to meet a unipony," Spike said.

They swam to the dead zone, where the coral was ghostly white. That's where the magical archway was that led to the river by the Enchanted Pony Academy. One by one, they swam through. Lana zoomed through a rush of bubbles and bobbed to the surface of the river.

Chapter 4

Lana saw a few ponies with sparkly hooves grazing near the riverbank. A pretty pink one looked up. "Marina! Hello!"

"Hi, Daisy! I brought some friends," Marina said.

Daisy and the other ponies trotted closer to the river. "Merchildren, too! How exciting."

"This is my partner, Lana, and her classmates," Marina said.

Lana was so dazzled by the beautiful pony, she could only wave hello.

Marina introduced Daisy to the rest of the merkids and seaponies. "And this is Spike!"

"Nice to meet you," Daisy said. "Are you a dolphin?"

Spike laughed. "I'm not sure what I am."

"That's why we're here," Marina explained. "We were hoping you might have books in your library about unique ocean animals." Marina looked at Lana, like she was waiting for her to finish explaining.

Lana cleared her throat. "Yes, because Principal Vanora thinks he's a rare species."

"I can check!" Daisy said.

"We also thought a unipony might know something about Spike," Nixie said. "Since they both have horns."

"Great idea! While I go to the library, say hi to Electra. She's one of the magical uniponies who live here. I'll be back in a flash!" Daisy ran off.

A pony with a rainbow mane and tail stepped closer to the river. She had a beautiful, glowing horn.

Spike swam closer. "I've never seen another creature with a horn."

"I've never seen a horn as long as yours!" Electra said. "Maybe we're related!"

"I'm so excited to meet someone like me," Spike said. "Even if you don't live in the sea."

Electra bent down, and they touched horns. They both giggled.

Lana was so happy to see Spike smiling.

The other magical ponies chatted with the merchildren and seaponies while they waited for Daisy. They shared apples from the trees.

"Look what I can do!" Cruise juggled three apples in the air.

Cali grabbed a handful and juggled four.

Prince Cruise tried to juggle five, but he dropped them all in the river. His seapony, Jetty, zoomed over to gobble them up. Everyone laughed.

Spike stabbed one with his horn, then tossed his head, sending the apple flying. The seaponies chased after it.

"We've got tons of apples. Take some home!" Electra told them.

Everyone gathered some of the delicious fruit.

"I bet Principal Vanora would like one," Lana said quietly to Marina.

"I'm sure she would!" Marina said.

Daisy quickly returned. "The librarian knew exactly the right book!" The pony cleared her throat to cast a spell. "Open the book so we can look!" The book floated out of her saddlebag and opened in front of her.

What wonderful magic! Lana thought.

The pages in Daisy's book turned until it opened to one with a picture of a creature just like Spike. "Listen to this!" she said. "*A rare type of whale called the narwhal often has what looks like a horn protruding from its head.*"

"I'm a whale?" Spike whispered. "A narwhal?"

"That's what the book says!" Daisy said.

"Can I see it?" Nixie asked.

"Sure!" Daisy used her magic to float the book closer to the river.

Lana frowned. She wanted to read about narwhals, too. But Nixie had asked first.

Nixie turned to the next page. "The horn is actually a tusk, or a long tooth!"

"That's the biggest tooth I've ever seen!" Prince Dorado said.

Spike proudly thrust his tusk in the air.

"Narwhals live in pods in the Northern Seas," Nixie went on.

"You're far from home," Marina said.

"Yeah. And I'm not a dolphin," Spike said. "I've been living with them all my life! I can't thank you all enough for your help."

The merchildren and seaponies said goodbye to the ponies and swam back through the magical portal. Lana loved how the tickly whoosh of bubbles felt as they swam through.

They went back to school and told the principal everything.

"A narwhal! How fascinating! And how lucky we are to have met you, Spike," Principal Vanora said.

"I'm the lucky one. I wouldn't know who I am without all of you," Spike said.

"It's a wonderful mission accomplished!" Principal Vanora said. "I'd say that earns you all early dismissal."

The class cheered.

Lana took a deep breath, trying to find the courage to hand her apple to the principal.

But the principal had another announcement. "Please be on the lookout for the lost trident and its gems we talked about last week. Since Nixie and her friends found the Sea Diamond recently, we believe the Trident of Protection, the big, pink Fathom Pearl, and the Night Star are out there, too. It would be wonderful to restore the trident's protective power to the Eastern Seas," the principal said. "We'll see you next weekend. Safe travels back home to your kingdoms."

"Would you like an apple?" Waverly asked the principal.

"How lovely! Thank you so much," the principal said.

Lana's shoulders drooped. She should have spoken up sooner so she could have given the apple to the principal. Slowly, she swam out of the school.

Spike and Marina followed.

"My kingdom is north of here," she told Spike, determined to be cheerful for his sake. "It's on the way to the Northern Seas.

Why don't you swim with us? You can spend the night at my castle."

"That would be great. Thanks!" Spike said.

They swam out of Astoria toward Lana's home. Finally, she had a break from Rescue Crew School!

Chapter 5

The beautiful castle where Lana's family lived soon appeared in the distance. It was built from chalky white clamshells and the deep blue shells of mussels. The water here in the north was colder than in Astoria.

The king and queen's seaponies were grazing in front of the castle. Lana waved to them, and they bobbed their heads at her.

Lana rushed into the castle. "I'm home! And I brought a friend!"

Her parents, King Keel and Queen Nerina, swam to the grand entrance. Her little sister, Tulia, followed.

"Welcome home!" Tulia said. "I missed you, and Marina, too."

"And this is Spike," Lana said. "He's a narwhal! He needs to find his pod."

"Hello!" Spike bobbed his head.

"Any rescue calls while I was gone?" Lana asked. Since all royal mermaids were on the Rescue Crew, her parents went out on calls, too. But they usually left the rescues to younger members like her cousins, Coral and Trent.

"No, it's been nice and quiet," her mother said.

"That's good." Lana didn't want to think about rescues for a long time. It was going to be a relief to work with her tutor on Monday, when she could focus on easier topics like Mer History and Care of the Seas. She had no problem speaking up with her tutor.

"Dinner is waiting in the dining room," her father said. "Your favorite! Shrimp stew."

"Yum! And look what I brought!" Lana plucked a few apples out of Marina's saddle-bag. "They're called apples. They're from the surface!"

"Wow!" Tulia said.

They all went to the dining room, and Lana and Marina told them all about their trip to visit the ponies.

"I hope I get to do that when I go to the rescue school," Tulia said.

"You've still got a few years before you start training," her mother reminded her.

"It sounds like things are going very well at Rescue Crew School," her father said.

Lana's smile disappeared.

The king frowned. "Is there a problem with your studies?"

Lana didn't want to disappoint her parents. "Everything's fine. There's so much to learn. And everyone else is so smart and brave."

"Lana just needs to speak up so everyone else can see how great she is," Marina said.

Lana flinched. She didn't want her family worrying.

Queen Nerina stirred her stew. "She's always been a quiet, dreamy merchild."

"Which aren't great qualities for a Rescue Crew member," Lana mumbled.

"Well, you sort of rescued *me*," Spike said.

"I wouldn't know who I am or where I come from without your help."

Lana looked down and blushed.

"So what will you do now, Spike?" Lana's father asked.

"I'm heading to the Northern Seas to find the other narwhals."

"When are you leaving?" Tulia asked.

"I'd like to go tomorrow morning. Now that I know I'm not the only one of my kind, I can't wait to meet others like me. I'm so excited!" Spike said.

"There's a portal a few miles north of here. It will take you right to the Northern Seas. It works just like the one you took to see the ponies," King Keel said.

Lana dropped her spoon. "There is? I didn't know that."

Her father nodded. "We've never used it, but it's part of the Stillwater territory. The portal is an archway made of coral."

"Just like the one to the river," Lana said.

"Are there other portals, besides those two?" Marina asked.

"There used to be one to the Western Seas," Queen Nerina said. "But it was destroyed in the Great Storm."

"Can we swim with Spike to the portal tomorrow?" Lana asked. "I'll have to miss classes with my tutor, but this will be educational." And it would be a great way to keep her mind off her Rescue Crew School worries.

"I want to go, too!" Tulia said.

"Of course. I bet Spike would appreciate the company," Queen Nerina said.

"That would be great," Spike said.

"Come on, let's go upstairs! Can we please be excused?" Lana asked.

"Yes, you may," her mother said.

They raced upstairs. Lana had decorated a beautiful room right next to hers for Marina. It was a tradition for Rescue Crew members to share their homes with their magical seapony partners.

Marina's room wasn't that big, though. Spike kept banging his tusk into things. "Maybe the other narwhals will have some advice on how to be less clumsy!" he joked.

I wish someone had some advice for me, Lana thought sadly. She was jealous that Spike was going to have a brand-new start. She sure could use a new start at the Rescue Crew School.

Chapter 6

The next morning, Lana clipped on her Say Shell in case she needed to communicate with any animals who didn't speak the Mer language. Then she, Marina, and Tulia headed off with Spike.

"I wonder if your dolphin family has been looking for you," Lana said.

"Probably not. I left a message that I was leaving. They know it's for the best," Spike said.

"Still, I'm sure they'd like to know you're okay," Marina said.

"Let's ask some of the animals of the kingdom to spread the word," Lana offered.

Tulia grabbed Lana's hand as they swam toward the portal. Lana gasped. "Look, it's a flotilla of sea turtles!"

"A flotilla?" Spike asked.

Lana nodded happily. "That's what a group of them is called."

"See, you know your schoolwork," Marina said.

"That was such an interesting lesson. And it definitely makes sense why a group of sharks is called a shiver!" Lana shuddered. "I shiver just thinking about them. But I'm not afraid of these turtles."

Tulia hid behind Marina. "They're so big!"

"Turtles are kind," Marina told her.

Lana swam up to them, grateful she was wearing her Say Shell. "Excuse me, have you seen a pod of dolphins looking for a lost member? For a dolphin with a horn, like my friend here?"

A turtle swam toward her. "My goodness, you're a member of the Royal Mermaid Rescue Crew! Are you on a mission?"

"No, I don't even have my rescue cape with me. We're just trying to get the word out that my friend Spike is going to meet up with the narwhals of the north," Lana explained.

"He thought he was a dolphin, but he's a narwhal!" Tulia said.

"We haven't seen any dolphins, but if we do, we'll let them know about Spike!" the turtle said.

"Thanks so much!" Lana said.

They swam on, giving the same message to a school of tuna and a great big humpback whale.

"Hopefully, someone will find the dolphins," Lana said.

"Thanks," Spike said. "You're such a great friend. And a great Rescue Crew member."

Lana didn't think that wasn't true, but she smiled anyway.

"Look, there's the coral archway!" Marina said.

"It's the portal!" Tulia said.

Spike paused.

"Aren't you going to go through?" Lana asked.

"I'm scared," Spike said. "Will you come with me?"

Lana bit her lip.

"Please?" he said. "You're on the Rescue Crew. Isn't this the sort of thing you do? Help sea creatures?"

"That's true," Tulia said.

Lana felt her chest tighten. She looked at Marina.

"He's got a point." Marina laughed. "Sorry, that wasn't a joke about your tusk."

Lana smiled. She was going to miss Spike. It would be nice to spend a little more time with him. "Okay, we'll come."

"Me too!" Tulia said.

"Sorry, kiddo. You're too little. Go home and tell Mom and Dad I'll be back in a few days."

Tulia crossed her arms and pouted. "I'm too scared to swim home all alone."

Tulia was too young to make the trip back herself. But Lana wanted Marina to come to the Arctic. It was too bad Tulia didn't have a rescue seapony yet.

But there was a seapony grazing nearby. Lana swam up to it. "Hello, what's your name?"

The seapony's eyes widened. "I'm Mobi. Are you a princess?"

"I am. And I'm a member of the Rescue Crew. I need your help."

"Of course. Anything!"

"Please escort my sister, Princess Tulia, back to our castle," Lana said.

"This will be good practice for when you're on the Rescue Crew," Marina told Tulia.

Tulia nodded and clapped her hands. "Let's go, Mobi!"

Lana watched them swim away.

"Another great solution," Marina said.

Lana shrugged. "But it wasn't a rescue. And the principal didn't see me do it."

"Are we ready to travel to the Arctic?" Spike asked.

"Let's go!" Marina said.

Chapter 7

Lana, Marina, and Spike swam under the arch and zoomed through a tunnel of bubbles, just like they had on the way to the river. But here, the water was getting colder and colder. They started slowing down and emerged from another archway into icy, blue waves.

The sandy ocean bottom was mostly barren. "There aren't any plants," Lana said, looking around. There were no bright corals like in Astoria and Stillwater and not very many fish. It was eerily quiet, except for the creaking and groaning of the ice around them. "I hope this is the right place."

They swam past a giant chunk of ice floating in the water. A school of fish flashed by, and a seal plunged into the water after them.

"I wonder where the other narwhals could be." Spike sounded worried.

"We'll keep looking until we find them," Lana said.

They swam along the edge of the ice for a while but still didn't see any other narwhals.

"The water sure is getting murky." Marina fluttered her fins and coughed.

"There's something up ahead," Lana said quietly. "It's moving."

"What is it?" Spike sounded scared.

As they slowly swam closer, Lana saw a walrus digging in the sand.

"Excuse me, I'm Princess Lana of the Royal Mermaid Rescue Crew. What are you looking for?"

"Lunch." He popped a clamshell into his mouth, swallowing it whole. "What are you looking for?"

"We're trying to find a pod of narwhals," Lana said.

The walrus gobbled another clam. "You'll find them in the open water. Swim away from the edge of the ice. And don't you touch these clams. I found them first."

"We won't. And thank you," Lana said.

They swam into deeper waters. A jelly-fish with tentacles ten times as long as Lana glided past them.

"That's the lion's mane jellyfish!" Lana said.

"You'll be able to draw a great picture for your assignment," Marina said.

They kept swimming, and Lana wondered where the narwhals could be.

"What if I can't find them?" Spike stopped swimming. He looked so sad.

"We can't give up now! Come on, let's keep going!" Lana said.

They swam on under the thick ice until the ice got thinner and they saw a big opening overhead. They popped up above the surface and saw a large stretch of open water.

Lana saw dark figures swimming in the distance. One with a long horn burst above the water. "Look! Narwhals!"

Spike smiled. "So the ponies were right. I'm really not the only one."

"They could be your family," Marina said.

"Let's go find out," Lana said.

They hurried over to the big group of narwhals breaching the surface. Chirps and whistles filled the water. As they got closer, a few of the creatures stared at them.

Spike cleared his throat. "Um, hi. Hello. My name is Spike."

"Hi, I'm Krill," said a small spotted narwhal. "How come we've never seen you before?"

Spike quickly explained everything that had happened in the last few days.

An older narwhal pushed past the others. "Star, is that you? Come here. Let me see you. You must be my lost baby! Do you have a star on your belly?"

Spike rolled on his back.

"Look, there's a star!" Lana said.

"Star! It's me, Maris! I'm your mother!" the older narwhal cried.

"I can't believe it! But what happened? How did you lose me?" Spike asked.

Spike's mom looked down and sighed. "It was my fault. We were chasing a school of halibut. The biggest school I'd ever seen. I was so excited, I rushed ahead, and I lost you. I looked for days, but we couldn't find you."

Lana felt so sad hearing the story.

"How did I end up with the dolphins?" Spike asked.

"There was a school of dolphins going after the fish, too. You must've gone off with them by mistake. You didn't have your tusk yet. I'm sure you blended in."

"I didn't even know I was a narwhal. I thought I was a misfit dolphin!" Spike said. "I can't believe I finally found my way home!"

"I can't believe it, either!" said his mother. "My Star is back!"

Spike paused. "Um, can we stick with the name Spike?"

"Of course, dear!" Maris said.

"Why don't you have a tusk?" he asked her.

"The females usually don't," his mom said. "But yours is beautiful."

Spike turned to Marina and Lana. "Thanks so much for helping me find my way home. I couldn't have done it without you."

"Did you come to visit the mermaids?" his mother asked Lana.

Mermaids? Lana was too stunned to say anything.

"There are mermaids here?" Marina asked.

Spike's mom nodded. "I can take you to them if you'd like."

Lana blinked a few times before she said, "Yes, please!"

Chapter 8

Spike's mom led them from the open water and dove under the ice. They swam until they came to the base of a huge glacier. An elaborate gate was carved into the milky white ice.

"This is Glister Kingdom," Maris explained. "All the merfolk live here, but they rarely venture far from the glacier."

"I wonder why," Lana said. "There's so much to explore in the ocean."

"I'm not sure. We don't interact with the merpeople very often."

Slowly, the gate lifted. Two mermen holding crystal staffs swam out.

"State the purpose of your visit," one of the men said.

Lana froze. She didn't know what to say. Luckily, Marina did.

"We're from the kingdom of Stillwater," the seapony explained. "This is Princess Lana, daughter of King Keel and Queen Nerina. We were escorting this young narwhal home when we learned there is a colony of mermaids here. We'd like to meet them."

Lana nodded. "That's right."

"Very well. We'll get the king and queen,"

one of the guards said before they both swam inside and closed the gate.

Lana turned to Marina. "Why doesn't anyone know merfolk live up here?"

"I have no idea. This is quite a discovery. Wait until you tell the principal," Marina said.

Lana frowned. She didn't want to think about the Rescue Crew School.

The gate opened again, and the king and queen swam out, followed by a mergirl around the same age as Lana and a merboy who looked to be about a year younger. They were all wearing crowns. Their skin had a pearly sheen, and their hair was brightly colored, similar to Lana's.

The queen swam toward them. "Hello. I

am Queen Yara, and this is King Marinus of the Glister Kingdom. These are our children, Princess Meri and Prince Hurley."

Lana surprised herself with how easily she said, "Hi, I'm Princess Lana of the Stillwater Kingdom. And this is my magical seapony partner, Marina."

"It's lovely to meet you," the king said. "I've always wondered if there were other merfolk in the sea."

Lana nodded. "There are lots of other merpeople in kingdoms all across the Eastern Seas."

"What brought you here?" the queen asked.

"We helped my friend Spike find his home." Lana started telling the story.

A loud noise from overhead interrupted her tale. Her eyes widened.

Boom! Boom! Boom! Boom!

A bell hanging from the side of the glacier started clanging.

"We must get inside at once!" the queen cried.

Merfolk appeared in the distance, swimming toward the glacier.

Boom! Boom! Boom! Boom!

Lana felt frozen in place. "What is that?" she whispered.

"I don't know, but let's go!" Marina said.

Princess Meri grabbed Lana's hand,

pulling her toward the castle. Before they slipped inside, Lana looked up and saw four huge black paws stalking across the ice above. It looked like they'd come crashing down on their heads at any moment!

Chapter 9

Merfolk flooded through the gates.

Inside, a small crystal city spread out in the hollow interior. A beautiful castle was nestled in the ice at the back of the glacier.

"Wow!" Marina said.

The booming outside continued. Lana wondered what kind of enormous creature was stalking overhead, sending panic throughout the kingdom.

The gate to the glacier started to close.

A mermaid shrieked. "No! My little Pasha isn't here. She was right behind me, but she's gone. Keep the gate open!"

"I'm sorry," one of the guards said. "We must keep it closed until the beast passes. We have to guard the kingdom."

"Someone help me!" the mermaid cried.

Marina looked at Lana. "We should look for the child."

"But Principal Vanora told me I can't lead a mission," Lana said.

"No one else from the Rescue Crew is here!" Marina said. "We have to help."

Lana hung her head. "Remember what happened last time a merchild went missing? I froze and did nothing."

"That's not true. You stopped and figured

out what happened. Let's go find that little mergirl!" Marina swam toward the gate.

Lana followed. Marina was right. They had to at least try. But she had no idea what they were facing. What kind of creature had paws that big?

Lana approached the king and queen. "Marina and I will search for the child. We are members of the Royal Mermaid Rescue Crew. It is our duty to keep the seas and its subjects safe."

"You don't even know this area," the king said.

"Do you have any experience with polar bears?" the queen asked.

"That's what's stomping around?" Lana asked.

"Yes. He may just pass overhead, but if he gets into the castle it would be a catastrophe," Queen Yara said.

"Then we have to find that child," Lana said. "Let us out."

The queen nodded at the guards. "Do as they say."

"I want to go with them," Princess Meri said.

Prince Hurley swam next to her. "So do I."

"Absolutely not!" the king said. "It's too dangerous. Lana and Marina are trained for this."

Lana and Marina swam out of the gate. But right before it closed, Meri and Hurley slipped out, too.

Boom! Boom! Boom! Boom!

The bear was still above them, but the noise seemed to be growing more distant.

"So what's the plan?" Hurley asked.

Lana looked around the still, icy waters.

"What should we do?" Meri asked.

"Hang on, I'm thinking." Lana floated there doing nothing, just like she had back at the park. *Breathe, focus, solve,* she reminded herself. This wasn't a game of hide-and-seek, like in the park, but she figured this mergirl had searched for a place to hide, too—the footsteps must have scared her into taking shelter.

"Are there any caves or places she might hide?" Lana asked Meri and Hurley.

Meri shook her head. "That's why

everyone rushed to the castle. And that's why we can't go far from home."

"So she must be nearby," Marina said.

"Do the polar bears swim below the ice?" Lana asked.

"Not often, but we must be careful," Meri said.

Lana turned circles in the water, looking for where she would hide if a polar bear was overhead. Nothing below the ice seemed like a decent hiding spot. "The ice above is a solid sheet?"

"Yes, on this side of the glacier," Hurley told her.

"What about the other side?" Lana asked.

"The ice starts to break up. There is some open water there," Meri said.

Lana looked at Marina.

"If there's no place to hide below the ice, maybe she's hiding above the ice. Let's swim to the other side of the glacier," Lana said.

Hurley crossed his arms. "I don't know. We rarely go over there."

"A scared mergirl might have ended up there without realizing it," Lana said. "We need to check." Lana swam around the glacier and Marina followed.

"We're coming, too!" Meri hollered.

The glacier was huge. It took a few minutes to swim around it. When they got to the other side, there were patches of open sea above. Small blocks of ice bobbed in the water.

"Maybe she climbed onto one of these." Lana poked her head above the water.

Seals sunned on a patch of ice nearby, some barking and chasing each other. Others flopped into the sea. Seabirds swarmed up into the sky. The water itself was a smooth sheet.

It was so beautiful and peaceful. But Lana couldn't get distracted. She had to find the mergirl. "Pasha! Where are you?"

Meri and Hurley popped their heads above the water. "Pasha! Let us help you. The bear is gone."

"I'm over here!" a faint voice called. The little mergirl was sitting on a small hunk of ice, waving her hands overhead.

"Come here, we'll take you back!" Meri called.

"I'm too afraid to get in the water!"

"Then we'll come get you!" Lana called. The four of them swam over to her.

Meri held out her hand. "Let's go home."

"What happened?" Hurley asked.

"When everyone was rushing toward the castle, I lost my mom. Then the gate closed. I wasn't sure what to do, so I just kept swimming as fast as I could. When I saw the ice chunks, I thought I might be safe from the bear up here," Pasha said.

"You're safe now," Lana said.

Meri helped Pasha into the water, and they headed back toward the gate.

Marina smiled at Lana. "You figured it out again."

"Well, it wasn't that hard," Lana said quietly.

"Lana, give yourself more credit. You led this mission and you found the mergirl! Principal Vanora would be so proud," Marina said. "You should be proud, too. And more confident. You're a great Rescue Crew member."

Lana was about to protest that she wasn't, that she should have been faster or braver. But she just smiled and said, "Thanks." Maybe she wasn't such a bad rescuer after all. She just wished everyone else knew it.

Chapter 10

When they got back to the other side of the glacier, the gate was open. Pasha's mom was waiting for her and gathered her into her arms.

Hundreds of merfolk waiting by the entrance cheered.

Spike spun in a circle. "You did it!"

His mother sighed. "If only someone had found you that quickly all those years ago."

"But I'm back now," Spike said.

"Thank you so much, Lana!" Pasha's mom wiped away her tears.

"Everyone helped," Lana said.

The queen gave her children a stern look. "You two shouldn't have swum off like that!"

"But Lana doesn't know the area!" Hurley said.

Meri crossed her arms. "We had to help."

"It's been a long day," the king said. "The sun will be setting soon, and we have something amazing to show you. But first, we'll feast."

"Spike and Maris, please join us as well," the queen said.

King Marinus led them to the castle dining hall, where they filled up on clams and kelp cakes.

"I'm surprised you could find any clams." Lana laughed. "We met a walrus nearby who seemed ready to eat them all!"

The queen raised an eyebrow. "They can get testy when our merchefs go harvesting."

"What do you eat where you live?" Meri asked Lana and Marina.

"Yeah, what's it like there?" Hurley asked.

Lana told them all about Astoria and Stillwater and the incredible sea life living in the coral reefs. She spoke for so long, and in such detail, that she surprised herself again. If she could speak up here, why couldn't she do it at the Rescue Crew School?

"It all sounds amazing!" Meri said.

Lana snapped her fingers. "You guys should train at the Rescue Crew School! All the royal merchildren are members of the Rescue Crew. And you two are royalty here in the Glister Kingdom. And your kingdom needs Rescue Crew members!"

"You'd get to choose your own magical seapony," Marina told them. "We're a great team."

"I've been to the rescue school," Spike said. "They're very nice. And they took me to the surface to meet magical ponies!" He told them all about it.

"Please, can we go, Dad?" Hurley asked.

Meri folded her hands, begging. "Please!"

Queen Yara shook her head. "It's so very far away. And we'd miss you."

"Rescue Crew School is only on weekends," Lana said.

"And there's a portal that transported us here very quickly," Marina explained.

"You could all come with us when we leave and check it out for yourself," Lana said.

Hurley and Meri were so excited, they swam in circles.

The king laughed. "We've never left the

kingdom. I didn't know about the portal. The queen can accompany the children. One of us has to stay here."

Hurley pumped one hand in the air. "Yes!"

"This is so exciting!" Meri hugged Lana.

"I think this is the perfect time to show our guests the magic in the sky," the queen said.

They swam out of the castle to an arch that opened up to the water. It was night, but the sky was covered in swirls of pale pink and blue and green. Lana gasped. "What is that?"

"The northern lights," the queen explained. "It looks a little different each night, but it's a beautiful way to end the day."

"It looks like your hair!" Spike said.

The king nodded. "Legend has it that our

first merfolk had pure white hair, until the night they gazed up at the northern lights," he explained. "The lights shone down on them, coloring their hair and leaving a shimmer on their skin. Just like we have. And like the streaks in your hair, Lana. I daresay you have some Northern Sea mermaid ancestors."

Lana grinned. Marina used her Sea Savvy to match the colors in the sky.

They sat on the ice and bobbed in the water, watching the sky for a long time. Lana felt so comfortable in the peaceful setting.

Later, Meri showed her and Marina to a guest room. Spike and his mom stayed over, too.

Lana had a hard time falling asleep. While the rescue that day had been a success, something else was bothering her. There were no places to hide in the kingdom. Maybe the merfolk could venture farther out and see more of the seas if they knew they had places to hide.

Lana sat up in bed. *I know what to do!*

Chapter 11

The next morning, Lana couldn't wait to share her plan during breakfast. "I've got an idea to help keep your kingdom safe, but we'll need buckets and buckets of clams."

Meri laughed. "How will clams keep us safe?"

Lana smiled. "You'll see."

After breakfast, Lana led her new friends to the spot where the walrus had been feeding. He was there again, snacking away.

"You better not be here for my food," he said.

"No, we're here to ask for help, and we've got loads of clams to give you in return," Lana said. "The merfolk need some small caves dug into thick patches of ice throughout the kingdom so they can hide if there's danger. You could use your tusks to help dig."

The walrus twitched his whiskers. "That sounds like a fair trade."

"Invite your friends," Meri said. "We have lots and lots of clams."

"I'll show you where to build the first one!" Lana said.

"We'll go get more clams," Hurley said.

Lana led the walrus to the location of the first cave. "We need a few made, so you could be busy all week."

"As long as you keep the clams coming, I'll be digging." The walrus started chipping away at the ice with his tusks.

"I'm sure the narwhals would be willing to help. We can use our tusks, too," Spike said.

"That would be great!" Meri said.

Lana showed Spike where to dig, and he and his mom swam off to find their pod.

"We can use clamshells to help dig," Meri said.

Marina smiled. "You're thinking like a Rescue Crew member already."

After they scouted out the perfect spot for a cave, the narwhals returned. Lana, Meri, Hurley, and a few other merfolk helped them carve out a cave.

Hurley dug into the ice. "This is such a great idea. And we can build even more after you leave."

"I'm so glad we met you." Meri hugged Lana.

Lana hugged her back and dropped

her digging shell. It sank into a dark crevice in the ocean floor. "Oh! There aren't any more clamshells."

"Let me try my magic," Marina said. "This is a spell to find the lost shell." But the shell didn't return. "Darn."

Lana patted Marina's neck. "Good try."

"See, we both still have things to work on," Marina said.

"I'll get it," Spike said. "I've always liked diving deep."

"No whale can dive deeper than a narwhal," his mother said proudly.

He disappeared into the depths of the ocean. In just a few minutes, he was back. He held the clamshell in his mouth and dropped it in Lana's hand. And there was a big, pink pearl, too!

Lana gasped. "What's this?"

"I remembered the story your principal told about the missing gems. That looks an awful lot like the Fathom Pearl she described," Spike said.

"It really does!" Marina said.

"I can't wait to show it to the principal," Lana said. And there was something else she wanted to tell the principal. An idea she had for helping the Rescue Crew. She hoped she could be brave enough to speak up and share her plan.

They spent a few more days in Glister Kingdom, carving caves into the ice.

"We need to leave. It's Friday. We'll go back to my kingdom, and then I can take you to Rescue Crew School on Saturday," Lana said.

"Let's pack our things, children. It's time for an adventure," the queen said.

When they were ready to leave, Spike and his mom swam with them to the portal.

"Please come visit soon," Spike said to Lana. "I'll miss you guys."

"You can always visit us, too," Lana said.

"It's a deal," Spike said.

Just then, a pod of dolphins rushed out of the portal. They looked around, confused. Then one spotted Spike. "Spike! A whale told us we might find you here. You shouldn't have run off like that!"

Spike hung his head. "I'm sorry, Mom." He paused. "Boy, is this confusing. Turns out, I'm not a dolphin with a horn. And I have another mom who I just found." Spike explained everything to the curious dolphins.

Maris swam up to the dolphins. "Thank you for taking such good care of my baby."

"He's a wonderful boy," Spike's dolphin mother said. "We miss him."

Lana had never seen Spike look so sad. The narwhal was blinking back tears.

"I miss you, too. But I'm a narwhal. I belong here."

His dolphin mother nodded sadly.

"Spike," Maris said softly. "There's no

reason you can't visit with your dolphin family."

"Really?" Spike said.

"You have this whole other pod who loves you. And you love them, too. How could I keep you apart?" Maris asked. "I just hope you'll spend time with your narwhal family as well."

"That sounds perfect!" Spike said.

"How about now, Spike?" one of the dolphins asked. "We found a huge school of cod on the other side of the portal."

"Don't get lost this time!" Maris laughed.

"Mom, why don't you come, too?" Spike asked her. "There are so many wonderful things to see."

"We'd love to have you," Spike's dolphin mother said.

Maris smiled. "Why not?"

Everyone swam through the portal, and moments later, they were back in Lana's kingdom. Spike, his moms, and the dolphins said goodbye, and went searching for the cod.

Lana brought everyone else to her home. Everything had turned out so well! But nerves bubbled in her belly knowing she'd be headed back to the Rescue Crew School soon.

Chapter 12

After spending the night at her family's castle, Lana led the group of Glister mer-royals to Rescue Crew School Saturday morning. There was so much to tell the class, but she was getting more and more nervous the closer they got to Astoria. Would she be in trouble for leading a mission? Would she be brave enough to tell the principal her idea?

"It certainly is warm down here," Queen

Yara said. "I'm not so sure you kids will like that."

"We'll get used to it!" Meri said.

They marveled at the bright coral and fish that appeared as they swam into the capital city.

Lana saw the school ahead and stopped swimming. "I'm scared."

Marina nudged her with her snout. "That's okay. Everyone feels scared once in a while. But you have so many great ideas, you have to share them. It's not fair to the group if you don't."

"But what if they laugh at me?" Lana asked.

Marina snorted. "Then ignore them. Or

laugh with them! But don't bottle up your words."

"Thanks, Marina. I couldn't have done any of this without you." She hurried toward the school, but she was a few minutes late for class. She burst through the door. "I'm sorry."

The principal sighed. "Princess Lana, you'd better have a good excuse."

The class gasped as the glittering royal family swam in behind her.

The principal set down her book. "Princess Lana, who are these merfolk?"

Everyone was looking at Lana. Her heart started pounding. Her cheeks were burning. She couldn't find her voice. She wished she could disappear.

"Well?" the principal asked.

Marina looked at Lana. "You can do this."

Lana shook her head. It was like her voice had vanished.

Marina sighed. "I can explain."

But Lana knew this was her moment. She had an exciting story to tell. She'd done well in the north. She'd found a missing merchild. She'd found an unknown colony of merfolk—and brought back the Fathom Pearl! She had to be proud and brave and tell the story.

Breathe, focus, solve. I can do this!

She cleared her throat. "Principal Vanora, class, I'd like to introduce the royal family of Glister Kingdom, from the waters of the Northern Seas."

Everyone gasped.

"Merfolk in the north!" the principal exclaimed. "How did you come to discover them?"

Lana took a deep breath and explained everything, then finished with, "I thought Meri and Hurley could train with us so they can keep their kingdom safe."

"Yeah, we want to be like Lana. She found a missing merchild while she was there," Meri said.

"She was amazing! She didn't just go searching for her. She stopped and figured out where the child would be, and she was right!" Hurley said.

"Is that so?" the principal asked.

"Yes," Lana said softly. "I know I wasn't supposed to lead a mission, but someone had to help."

Principal Vanora paused. Lana gulped, ready to be scolded.

"I'm very proud of you," the principal said.

"Really?" Lana's heart swelled.

"Really. And we'd be thrilled to have Meri and Hurley join us," the principal added. "Why don't you find seats and start today?"

"Excellent! I'll see you two after class," the queen said before swimming off.

"This has been quite a morning!" the principal said. "Let's take a quick break."

As the merchildren swam off into the courtyard, Lana approached Principal Vanora. "Can I talk to you about something?"

"Of course," the principal said.

Her heart fluttered and her skin felt prickly, but she wasn't going to keep her words and ideas bottled up anymore. "I know I'm not quick to act. I know I have a hard time speaking up, but I want you to know that I'm working on it."

"I can see that," the principal said.

Lana took a deep breath. "I like spending time thinking, solving problems. It's what I'm good at." She told the principal about the ice caves they'd been building.

"It sounds like you did a good job up there," the principal said.

Lana nodded. "I think we should make a new position on the Rescue Crew—a project planner. Solving problems that aren't emergencies. I've already got some ideas for us down here in Astoria."

The principal placed her hand on Lana's shoulder. "I think that's a wonderful idea. And I'm so glad you were brave enough to share it with me."

Lana gasped. "I almost forgot. I've got something else to share with you." She reached into her schoolbag and pulled out the pearl. "Spike found this while we were digging the caves. Do you think it's the Fathom Pearl?"

The principal held it in her hand. "Fathom

pearls are very rare. But the one in the trident was the only pink one ever discovered. We won't know until we can put it in the missing trident, but I think this could be it!"

Lana beamed. "I hope so!"

"I'm so glad you found this—and your confidence. They're both treasures."

Lana smiled at Marina. "Like you said, a team takes two. And luckily, Marina convinced me that I have a lot to share."

Lana wrapped her arms around Marina's neck, glad they were back at the Rescue Crew School. Where they belonged.

The adventures continue . . .

Mermaids TO THE RESCUE

#3: Cali Plays Fair

Princess Cali and her twin brother, Prince Cruise, are expected to do everything together—but at the Royal Mermaid Rescue Crew School, Cali wants to stand out on her own. So when the principal announces a Rescue Crew tournament that will decide the top merstudent of the year, Cali is thrilled. This is the perfect way to prove herself!

But Cruise is a tough competitor. Will Cali do *anything* to win . . . even something fishy?

Welcome to the
ENCHANTED PONY ACADEMY,
where dreams sparkle and magic shines!